NiNA SONi

FORMER BEST FRiEND

For Rupa, whose childhood antics
inspired this book. —K. S

Ω

Published by
PEACHTREE PUBLISHING COMPANY INC.
1700 Chattahoochee Avenue
Atlanta, Georgia 30318-2112
www.peachtree-online.com

Text © 2019 by Kashmira Sheth
Illustrations © 2019 by Jenn Kocsmiersky

First trade paperback edition published in 2020

Edited by Kathy Landwehr
Copy edited by Amy Sproull Brittain
Design and composition by Adela Pons
The illustrations were rendered digitally

Printed in August 2020 by LSC Communications in Harrisonburg, VA
10 9 8 7 6 5 4 3 2 1 (hardcover)
10 9 8 7 6 5 4 3 2 1 (trade paper)
HC ISBN 978-1-68263-057-0
PB ISBN 978-1-68263-205-5

Library of Congress Cataloging-in-Publication Data

Names: Sheth, Kashmira, author. | Kocsmiersky, Jenn, illustrator.
Title: Nina Soni, former best friend / written by Kashmira Sheth ; illustrated by Jenn Kocsmiersky.
Description: Atlanta : Peachtree Publishing Company Inc., [2019] | Summary: Organized but sometimes forgetful Nina has a lot to keep track of as she rushes to complete a school project, help with little sister Kavita's birthday party, and make up with best friend Jay.
Identifiers: LCCN 2019006229 | ISBN 9781682630570
Subjects: | CYAC: Best friends—Fiction. | Friendship—Fiction. | Sisters—Fiction. | Family life—Fiction. | East Indian Americans—Fiction.
Classification: LCC PZ7.S5543 Ni 2019 | DDC [Fic]—dc23 LC record available at *https://lccn.loc.gov/2019006229*

NINA SONI
FORMER BEST FRIEND

Written by **Kashmira Sheth**
Illustrated by **Jenn Kocsmiersky**

PEACHTREE
ATLANTA

CHAPTER ONE

"What's so great about going fishing every weekend?" I asked Jay, waving my paintbrush.

Crash! My "asking hand" knocked over his pirate ship. It flung green paint from my brush too. Unlike Jay's pirate ship pieces, the paint splattered quietly. "Sorry, sorry, sorry!" I picked up the pieces of the captain's head and a prisoner's arm from the floor.

The whole class stopped what they were doing to stare at us.

"Nina, why can't you be more careful?" Jay's green

eyes, the color of bitter melon, were full of anger. My triple apologies seemed to have had no effect.

"Sorry," I whispered again. "I didn't mean to. Honest. I talk with my hands waving here and there—that's the way I am."

"That's just an excuse for being careless and ruining my ship," he said.

"You know how Kavita always sings, right?" Kavita is my little sister who makes up songs.

"Yeah."

"And my hands always move when I talk, right?"

No answer.

Even more when I am nervous, I wanted to say. But I did not; instead I waited for Jay to say something. Anything.

Silence.

"Right?" I repeated. "Hey. I didn't mean to knock down your ship and I'm sorry. Really sorry."

I don't think I had ever used six sorrys in two minutes before. That's three sorrys per minute. I thought that was an excellent apology.

Mr. Hays walked over. "What is going on here?" he asked.

Then he saw the sunken—I mean broken—ship,

headless pirates and prisoners, and splotches of green paint. His mouth flew open.

Other kids came closer. They gawked and gasped.

I wanted to hide under the table. On the floor, next to the broken pieces of Jay's ship.

"Everyone, go back to your own projects," Mr. Hays said.

I picked up a chunk of clay from the floor. I think once upon a time it was the captain's cabin. "I'm sorry, Mr. Hays. It was an accident."

He put his arm around Jay's shoulders. "It was a beautiful ship, Jay. I'm glad I saw it before it was broken. You will get an A."

That made me smile. "Thank you, Mr. Hays."

Jay was silent, staring at his broken ship and pirates.

Mr. Hays said, "Accidents happen, but try to be more careful, Nina."

"I will." I turned to Jay. "See? You still get an A. So no worries, right?"

Jay shot me a look that said *shut up*. He would have said it out loud if Mr. Hays wasn't around.

Jay and I cleaned up the mess and wiped green paint from the floor. But he didn't say a word to me.

I guess I haven't had very good luck with Jay Davenport lately. Until almost now he was my best friend. He used to come over all the time with his mom, or without her, to just hang out with us. We made squishy dough, rolled rotis, slathered them with buttery ghee after they were cooked, and ate them. While Mom worked on her landscape projects, we sat at the dining table and drew our own gardens and colored them. I loved going to his house and playing with all the blocks and building sets that belonged to his dad when he was young.

Then Jay's cousins moved here from California and Texas. So Jay got busy with them. On weekends, he went fishing with his grandpa and had sleepovers with his cousins, and every Thursday they had a big family dinner.

I saw him at school.

Side by side, we had talked and worked in our art class for six weeks. It was fun. His pirate ship was perfect. And now I had crashed it.

Would that sink our friendship too?

Two days later, when all the best projects were displayed, I felt really bad. Not because my swing set was not one of them. Because Jay's pirate ship would have been the best one if I hadn't crashed it.

The day we were supposed to take our clay sculptures home, Jay didn't come to school. I wondered if he didn't come because he had nothing to take home.

It made me sad, but I didn't know what to do.

✱✱✱

Jay and I were best friends.

This is my in-my-head list of the reasons why. An in-my-head list is a list I make in my head. Sometimes my head forgets part of the list, but I never forget to carry my head. And I don't need a paper, pen, or pencil for an in-my-head list.

My in-my-head list for why Jay and I were best friends

* Jay's mom, Meera Masi, and my mom are best friends.

* We're both Indian American—well, Jay is only half Indian. Just like Jay's mom, both of my parents came here from India. Jay's great grandfather came from Europe. Just like Jay, his grandfather and father were born right here in Wisconsin.

* Jay lives on my street.

* He's in my class.

* I see Jay at school, at neighborhood gatherings, and at Indian parties on weekends.

✳ He knows more than he should about
my family. Like when I was five, I wore
his mom's shoes and tumbled down the
staircase. Or that I hate bitter melon but
my mom makes me eat a few bites of it.
And the worst of all, on my first sleepover
at his house I cried and cried. Finally, my dad
had to come and get me at midnight.

Jay knows about my forgetfulness too.

For-get-ful-ness means your mind becomes so full
of new thoughts and ideas that it pushes out the
old ones.

It happens to me a lot. Now that Jay was not
my best friend, I wished he would forget about my
forgetfulness.

After the pirate ship accident, Jay didn't walk with me to school and didn't talk to me in class except to tease me. He made fun of things like me wearing a coat on a 70-degree day or never buying school lunch except on pizza Friday. When his mom came over to our house, he went fishing with his cousin Jeff and Grandpa Joe instead of coming too.

Maybe Jeff was his best friend now. Jeff wasn't clumsy. He didn't break Jay's pirate ship, ruin his art project, and make him sad.

I guess it was all my fault.

Still, it made me miserable to think that maybe Jay Davenport was my former best friend.

For-mer means once-upon-a-time.

CHAPTER TWO

It was a week and one day after the pirate ship mishap.

Mis-hap means an unlucky accident.

It was an unlucky accident for Jay. And for me too.

I was thinking about it when Ms. Lapin reminded us about our Personal Narrative Project.

"Class, you've had more than a week to work on your PNP, so I hope you're almost done with it. You will have tomorrow and Sunday to finish." She pointed to the assignment written on the whiteboard.

* Your Personal Narrative Project should be about three pages long.
* Identify a special event from your own life, like a special family gathering, a research project, an adventure, a trip, or any other experience. Describe it in detail and what you learned from it.
* Make sure your PNP includes an introduction of the event, then your observations about it, and finally your reactions.

I groaned. I had completely forgotten the PNP.

"Can it be a trip to Mars and back?" Luke asked.

"Mars?" Tyler whispered. "You've never been to Mars."

"So?"

"Luke, write about something you have experienced," Ms. Lapin continued. "That way you can describe what you learned. What did you find out about yourself or the people around you? Whatever your piece is—funny, happy, sad, scary, or adventurous—make sure it is in your voice. That means it should read like you're telling a story. Your PNP is due Monday."

I raised my hand.

"Yes, Nina."

"Can our observations be a list?"

"Certainly, as long as it consists of all that you noticed. If it was funny, what made it funny? What made you laugh? If it was amazing, what was so amazing about it?"

I was glad Ms. Lapin said I could make a list of my observations. I really, really enjoy making lists.

List making is

1. quick
2. organized
3. official looking
4. useful
5. fun

Maybe it isn't fun for everyone. But it is for me.

Sometimes my lists are in my head and sometimes I write them in my notebook. I have named my notebook Sakhi. People name their pets, their boats, and sometimes even their houses, so I decided to name my notebook Sakhi.

Sakhi means friend in Hindi.

My notebook is a good friend.

Mom says I like lists because I have a single-track

mind. I guess my mind is like a train and my ideas and thoughts are like the tracks. If something comes up, my mind gets on that track and follows it. I make a list about it. I focus so much on one thing that I don't pay attention to anything else.

Until something else comes up. Then I change tracks, shift my focus, and roll down that new track. And then I forget the first thing, or the second thing.

That's when I sometimes get in trouble. Sometimes I leave the old track before I reach my destination.

Des-ti-na-tion means where you are going.

This is what happened. I had already veered off the PNP track. (Because the completed PNP should have been my destination.) I got busy doing something else, like worrying about Jay's pirate ship crash, about him being mad at me, about my being clumsy, and about the possible end of our friendship. And I completely forgot about my PNP until Ms. Lapin reminded us.

Two weeks ago when Ms. Lapin gave us the assignment, I was on the PNP track. I thought and thought about what I could write. I tried to make a list of things I could write about. With my nothing-ever-happens family, I couldn't come up with even a single personal narrative idea. But I did make a list about my family!

Here is the list I made.

My family is

1. boring
2. the most regular kind
3. the ordinary type
4. one in which nothing ever happens

Conclusion: My life is about as exciting as a rice cake—bland.

> *Con-clu-sion* means what you have learned—in this case what I've learned from observing my family.

There are four of us in our family

1. My mom

2. My dad

3. My little sister, Kavita

4. And one more person. Oh yes, myself!

On top of being a super ho-hum family, we are a small family. (That is because my grandparents, aunts, uncles, and cousins live thousands of miles away in India.) Four people may not seem small, but if you take Mom and Dad out (and you have to because nothing exciting happens to parents), that leaves only Kavita and me.

And believe me, most of the time I could do without the excitement called Kavita. Why? Because Kavita's excitement is my embarrassment.

Em-bar-rass-ment means you wish you were a giant tortoise, so you could hide in your shell and pretend to be a rock.

On top of everything, for the past six months our family has shrunk from 4 to 3.3 people. Why? Because Dad has an assignment that takes him to Boston every week. We live in Madison, Wisconsin, and Boston, Massachusetts, is many states away. All week he is missing.

Here is a list of the number of people in our house each day

1. Monday: 3

2. Tuesday: 3

3. Wednesday: 3

4. Thursday: 3

5. Friday: 3

6. Saturday: 4

7. Sunday: 4

Total of all 7 days: 3+3+3+3+3+4+4= 23

23 people ÷ 7 days = 3.2857

3.2857 is almost 3.3

That's why we have 3.3 people in the family right now. If you'll notice, even 3.3 is a boring number.

I have lived with my family for nine years, so I'm used to them. I'm used to boring. It's never been a big deal. Until now. Now it is a big deal because I have to come up with my PNP and they are no help.

If my family were not so ho-hum, I wouldn't be in this predicament.

Pre-dic-a-ment means mess.

I like to use the word *predicament* because *mess* sounds like something Kavita gets into. I am older, so I get into predicaments.

"My PNP is about the day our dog barfed on the carpet," Tyler said. Without raising his hand.

"Is that the most exciting thing that's happened to you in nine years? Your life stinks," Luke said.

Ms. Lapin turned around. "Tyler and Luke!"

That was enough to quiet them.

A hand shot up to my left.

"Yes, Jay?" Ms. Lapin asked.

"I'm doing a story about how my cousin Jeff and I fished our grandpa out of Lake Mendota."

That Jay Davenport! I am sure he has used figurative language, and is probably already done with his project!

I wish I had a big family that did fun stuff with me. Like my grandpa falling into a lake and needing my rescue.

> **Res-cue** means to save.

If I had rescued my grandfather, I would have something to write about too.

Ms. Lapin said, "Very good. I hope all of you have come up with wonderful ideas like Jay's. Now let's start on science."

I wished I at least had an idea for my PNP. If I had a dog, even a barfing one like Tyler's, I could have come up with a PNP. But I don't even have a pet gerbil. Which means not having the chance to lose Ginger and search for her. (Ginger is the name I'd like for my pet cat, but I knew I wasn't getting one so I'd rather give that name to my gerbil, which I also don't have.)

Jay leaned over and whispered, "Miss Methodical, what's your list-making PNP about?"

In the past Jay has called me Miss Tidy, Miss Organized, and Miss Orderly. This was his fourth nickname for me. They all mean the same thing.

Jay knows I'm forgetful and make lists to keep myself on track. Whenever I talk about my lists he teases me with a new nickname.

Luckily, before I could answer him, Ms. Lapin asked us a science question. "How many of you have heard about antibiotics?"

Almost every hand went up.

"In 1928, penicillin was discovered," Ms. Lapin said. "The man who discovered this important antibiotic was named Alexander Fleming."

Then she told us that Fleming wasn't even looking for penicillin when he discovered it. He was working with bacteria and noticed mold growing in a petri dish. The mold had killed the bacteria around it. It led to the discovery of penicillin that saved millions of lives. She turned around to write on the whiteboard.

"Just like you, Jay, some people have all the luck in the world," I mumbled.

"Like my pirate ship crashing?" Jay whispered. "I'm never lucky."

He *had* been unlucky with the pirate ship. And it was my fault. But how could Jay say he was never lucky? He sees his family all the time. Plus, his dad doesn't have to be 1,139 miles away all week. (That's how far Boston, Massachusetts, is from Madison, Wisconsin.) And that's why he had no problem writing his PNP. That is an enormous amount of luck.

E-nor-mous means it *(E)* is not *(nor)* a mouse *(mous)*.

Enormous is not a mouse, it is as big as an elephant. Jay's luck was as big as an elephant.

"Alexander Fleming was observant," Ms. Lapin said. "He asked questions when he saw something unusual."

I raised my hand.

"Yes, Nina?"

"Like Newton when he saw an apple fall from a tree. He thought about why the apple came down, and not up. That is how he figured out gravity."

Ms. Lapin smiled sweetly. "Exactly."

That made me happy—like when Mom makes me a snack of spicy, sweet-and-sour chaat when I'm patient with Kavita, even when Kavita is singing away while I'm trying to do my homework. And my sister, she sings a lot. Always at the top of her lungs too.

Jay mouthed the words, "Teacher's pet."

I gave him a smug look. "Just like you were five minutes ago?"

✳✳✳

After class, Jay said to Tyler, "My PNP is going to be the best."

"Ha ha," I said without thinking.

"Nina thinks she'll beat you," Tyler said.

"I never said that. I was—"

"Oh yeah? Why were you laughing, Nina?" Tyler asked. "You don't think anyone can do better than you?"

"So, smarty-pants Nina, what's your PNP about?" Jay asked.

I stomped my foot and accidentally stubbed my toe on the chair leg. "Stop calling me smarty-pants!"

I had no clue what I was going to write about. I was worried about it, but there was no reason to tell Jay and Tyler that. If they found out that I'd forgotten about the PNP, they'd laugh at me. I had to come up with something quickly.

Something brilliant.

Doing better than Jay was very important to me. Even when we had been best friends (because I didn't think we were now), we competed. We just kept it secret from everyone else. Now our best-friendship days might be over, but that didn't mean our serious-competition days were.

Even if my life was boring, I had to come up with the most wonderful PNP.

I just had to.

"You don't even know what you're going to write about?" Tyler asked.

I thought about Alexander Fleming and his discovery. I guess because Ms. Lapin had just talked about it, I was still on the Alexander Fleming track. And Ms. Lapin had said we could write about a research project.

Jay stared at me, waiting for me to answer.

A brilliant idea flashed into my head. "I'm doing a story about my own discovery," I said.

"Wow!" Tyler looked impressed.

Jay gave me a sharp look. "What discovery?"

I looked away. "It's a secret."

No need to tell him that my discovery was still a secret from me too.

Tomorrow I had a dance class in the morning and Kavita's birthday party in the afternoon. That left only this evening and part of Saturday for my discovery, because I needed Sunday to write my report.

I didn't have a minute to waste.

CHAPTER THREE

On the way home, I took extra long steps. It usually takes me three steps to cross a concrete sidewalk slab, and today I did it in two. And I never once stepped on a crack.

Left, right, one slab.

Left, right, two slabs.

Left, right, three slabs.

All the way home.

I wondered if the stuffed eggplant Mom had made last week was still in the refrigerator. I loved the tiny eggplants filled with coconut and peanuts. But maybe they were too old to eat. Maybe they were growing mold. Like penicillin! What if it turned out to be a super-mold—a mold that could cure diabetes and maybe even cancer?

I could name it Ninacillin.

At home, Mom opened the door. She said something, but I didn't hear it. I headed straight for the kitchen. My fingers wiggled to open the refrigerator.

Mom followed me. "Where is Kavita?"

"Huh?"

"Your sister. Why didn't Kavita come in with you?"

This was not the great discovery I was hoping for.

Kavita was probably still at school with her teacher, Mrs. Jabs, singing away. Or maybe she was all alone and crying, wondering why I had left her at school.

"Oh, um, I'll get her right away." I dropped my backpack in the kitchen and took off. I felt worse than when I broke Jay's pirate ship.

"She's still at school?" Mom's shrill voice crawled up my back.

I didn't want to take the time to answer, and she kind of already knew the answer anyway. So I sprinted the two blocks back to school.

Kavita was supposed to be waiting on the bench

right inside the front door, just like she did every afternoon. But she wasn't there. I kept going down the hallway. Luckily, no one was around to scold me for running.

By the time I burst into Mrs. Jabs's classroom, I was huffing like a dragon in a Chinese New Year parade. I expected Kavita and her teacher to be waiting for me, but the room was empty. Even Mrs. Jabs was missing.

Quickly I checked out the other first-grade classrooms. Kavita wasn't in any of them.

Kavita loves the jungle gym at school. During summer break when we can go to any park in the city, she still wants to go to our school playground only because of the jungle gym.

Next stop, playground.

As soon as I got out there and called out, "Kavita! Kavita!" I realized there were still a few fourth- and fifth-grade boys hanging out on the playground. Including Jay.

"Hey, Nina, forgot your sister again?" he asked.

I rolled my eyes. *"Again?"*

He smirked. "Remember the first day of school?"

But the first day wasn't my fault at all. Dad was supposed to pick Kavita and me up from school, but he didn't remember the right time. He wanted to be home for the first day of school so he didn't go to Boston, and then he was late! After waiting for fifteen minutes, I went home; my sister did not.

I think that should count as Dad forgetting Kavita and me, not me forgetting Kavita.

But I didn't want to explain all that to Jay. Besides, I needed to find Kavita now. "Yeah, whatever you say. Have you seen her?"

"Nope."

"Has anyone seen her?" I even looked at the fifth graders when I asked. They didn't answer.

Mom rushed up to the schoolyard. Her eyes were as round as her roti. "Kavita *kahan hai?*"

"I don't know where Kavita is yet," I replied.

She asked. "*Mai sochi* you were looking for her. Why are you standing around *ladko ke saath*?" Her voice was panicky. Panicky sounds the same in Hindi as it does in English so I bet all the boys knew she was upset.

"I'm not just standing around with boys. I was asking them about Kavita."

So what did she do but ask those boys the same question I had. "Have you seen Kavita?"

They shook their heads. Jay said, "I didn't see her waiting on the bench outside like she usually does until Nina shows up."

"Thanks, Jay," Mom said. "Kavita still must be in her classroom."

"I looked, Mom. She's not there."

"We will look again."

"You check her classroom," I suggested. "I'll go to the cafeteria."

But there was nothing in the cafeteria except the icky smell of string beans from lunch. The long tables were clean and empty. It was one big, spooky, smelly, silent space.

On my way back to Mrs. Jabs's classroom, I took a detour and checked out the gym and the principal's office. Along with Kavita and her teacher, the principal was also missing.

Where was my sister? My stomach went queasy. I felt like I was going to throw up. I guess that's why they call it "worried sick."

CHAPTER FOUR

The door to the teachers' lounge was slightly open. I peeked inside. It was messy—an unfolded newspaper was on the table and grapes were on the floor. That kind of surprised me because:

1. Teachers are adults, so they know all about being clean.

2. Teachers ask their students to be clean and tidy.

3. Teachers should follow their own advice.

4. That means teachers should be clean and tidy.

But all the teachers had vanished, which meant they made a mess and didn't clean it up.

As I stepped back from the door, I saw a butt sticking out of the teachers' lounge trash can.

When you live with your sister all her life, you recognize her face, hands, and even her butt. I recognized that butt, so I swatted it. "Kavita! How did you get in here?"

"I came in to ask for help because I didn't see you. Nobody was here." Her trash-can voice was muffled.

"Let's go," I said.

"Wait! There's something shiny in the trash can. I want it."

I grabbed Kavita by the waist and pulled her out. Her green sweatshirt was covered with bits of banana goop and stained brown and yellow; her chin had an orange spot. Popcorn clung to her knitted hat that was pulled down over her ears.

"Look at you!" I said.

"Nina!" She pointed. "A diamond!"

I peered into the trash can. "I don't see anything shiny in there."

"It's under that gooey brown stuff. Pull it out, pull it out! I want to wear it for my party!"

"Yuck! I don't want to." I stepped back. Then a tiny voice in my head said, *Fleming wasn't afraid of mold. If you worry about yuck, you won't discover anything.* "Okay, fine. Let's tip this over."

Kavita and I tilted the trash can. A half-used packet of salad dressing fell out on my arm. Something yellow and sticky rolled out to the edge—maybe lemon filling or something that wasn't even food.

Luckily, nothing landed on the floor.

Then Mr. Bumbee, the school janitor, came in.

Kavita pointed at the tilted trash can. "Come, come, come, Mr. Bumbee! There's a diamond in here."

Mr. Bumbee looked at us like he had never met us before. Then he straightened the can with his gloved hand. He reached in and pulled out the diamond. It had turned into tinfoil.

Mr. Bumbee laughed.

Kavita laughed.

I couldn't laugh. I was busy wiping the salad dressing off.

I headed straight for the girls' bathroom and ran into Mom on the way. Her face was all crumpled up, like the tinfoil Mr. Bumbee had just pulled out of the trash can. Before she could ask about Kavita, I pointed toward the teachers' lounge.

Mom turned around just as Mr. Bumbee and Kavita walked out the door. Mom's bracelets jingled as she rushed towards them.

"You better wash your hands and face," Mr. Bumbee whispered to me.

Yuck! I ran into the bathroom. Luckily, nobody was there.

When I came out, Mom was hugging Kavita. "Mom, she's giving you germs!"

Mom kept on hugging. Usually she asks us to wash our hands before eating and when we come in from playing in the park, to get rid of the germs. But today, Mom had turned germ friendly.

"She was inside a trash can," I said, but Mom still didn't push Kavita away. "She was covered in peels. She's probably still covered in some nasty, gooey, goop."

I guess worries of Kavita made Mom's worries of germs disappear.

Hugging Kavita and her germs even made Mom smile. "Nina, everything is all right." Mom patted my head with the same germ-covered hand that had just been touching Kavita.

"What's that brown stuff on the side of your nose?" Kavita asked me.

Mom looked at me. Before she could say anything, I ran back to the bathroom.

I looked in the mirror.

There was nothing stuck on the left side of my nose.

There was nothing on the right side of my nose.

There was nothing on top of my nose.

Or even *in* my nose.

I ran back out. "Kavita!"

She walked over to Mr. Bumbee, who was down the hallway, and jingled his keys that were hanging from his belt. "Happy October Fools' Day, Nina!"

"There's only April Fools' Day," I said.

"But I fooled you in October, so it's October Fools' Day."

"You still have popcorn from the trash stuck on your hat." I said. "Take it off."

She held on to her hat with her hands. "NO!"

"Ready, Nina?" Mom asked. Then she turned to Mr. Bumbee. "Thank you for finding my daughter."

Mom usually is very observant but right now she was not.

> Ob-ser-vant means looking around and noticing everything.

"Mom, Mr. Bumbee didn't find Kavita, I did," I pointed out.

"Sorry, I thought he found her."

Mom held Kavita's hand with one hand; she put her other arm around me. The nasty stuff that she had picked up from Kavita was rubbing off all over me. As soon as I got home I was going to wash my hands and my hair.

But not my sweater. I would let germs grow on it. Maybe, if I were very lucky, some super-mold would develop and I could use it for my Personal Narrative Project. Then my PNP problem would be solved.

I wondered how quickly the mold would grow, probably not by tomorrow.

Maybe I should let the mold grow while I worked on other PNP project ideas. That way I would let the mold have all the time to grow, while I get my work done.

As we walked home, I realized I had already lost more than an hour. This was not a good Personal Narrative Project beginning.

My head filled with a song. *Hurry, hurry, hurry and get started on your PNP.*

It sounded a lot like Kavita's singing. Maybe I was spending too much time with her.

CHAPTER FIVE

"Dibs on the bathroom," I announced as we entered the house. I wanted to clean up quickly so I could get to my discovery.

In the shower I washed my hair and scrubbed my arms again to get rid of the salad dressing smell.

As soon as I was done with the bathroom, Mom took Kavita in for a shower.

I tossed my sweater in the back of my closet. Dad and Kavita were in charge of laundry. They never looked in my closet. Dad always asked me to bring my laundry down. And if Mom found my sweater, I could just pretend I forgot to give it to him.

I was going to give my sweater a week or two to grow mold and hope it could become a Ninacillin-sweater.

What *could* I use for my PNP?

The stuffed eggplant might still be in the refrigerator!

I hurried to the kitchen. The eggplant had disappeared. Mom must have eaten it or thrown it out before the mold could grow on it.

Even though Mom's nose was only a little bump, it was a mighty sniffer. We never had anything spoiling in our refrigerator or on the counter. That's why we weren't Alexander Fleming–type discoverers.

I checked a few bottles on the refrigerator's door shelf to see if anything was growing in any of them. One by one I opened and sniffed the hot chili pickle, coconut milk, spicy mango and lemon pickle, cayenne pepper sauce, and spicy mint chutney. I didn't see anything growing, but now my nose was twitchy, itchy, and sneezy.

I went back to my room and sat at my desk, pondering the PNP.

> *Pon-der* means to really think and think and think about something until your head is all pounded out with pondering.

Nothing came to my mind.

Maybe I was pounding my brain with too much pondering.

So I stopped pondering and started writing in Sakhi.

Steps to making a great discovery

I. Observe and don't be afraid of messy and gross things. A great discovery might grow in them.

2. If you see something different, ask questions. (No need to raise your hand to ask
   questions. And ask as many questions as you
   want.)
3. Out of old and gross, find something new and
   exciting.

Then I pondered a bit more about what things I could observe.

I had seen a lot of colorful leaves on the lawns and sidewalks. Do the colors wash away in the rain like washable markers or do they stay on like permanent markers?

There was an old yellowed bar of soap that had fallen between the washer and dryer in the laundry room. Could I wash the leaves with it and see what happens?

There was Mom's old lipstick I had taken when I was five. It was still in my secret drawer. Could l use that for a discovery? Like coloring the leaves with lipsticks and washing them with that yellowed bar of soap?

One of these things alone or combined might lead me to my new discovery. I wrote more in Sakhi.

Observation list

1.	colorful leaves
2.	old yellowed bar of soap
3.	lipstick in my secret drawer

What else, what else? I asked myself.

Bang, bang, bang! on my door. It was so loud that it had to be Kavita.

"I'm busy," I said.

The door opened. Mom peeked in. She looked as red as my scrubbed arms. "I've been calling you for the last five minutes. Please come and help me."

I followed her to the bathroom.

"Look at Kavita's hair," Mom said. "Gum. I didn't see it until I took off her hat and started washing her hair."

Kavita's hair was dripping. A huge pink blob was stuck on the top left side of her head. The hair underneath and all around was tangled up with it.

"*That's* why you didn't want to take your hat off at school," I said to Kavita.

Mom sighed. "I don't know what to do. We need to take care of this before her party tomorrow."

"Cut it off," I said.

Mom sighed. "No. There will be a bald spot."

"It'll grow back," I said.

Kavita shouted, "I'm good at hiding things! I'll cover my head until my hair grows back. I won't let anyone at my party see my bald spot."

Mom shook her head. "No, Kavita. We aren't cutting off your hair." She turned to me. "Nina, please call Meera Masi. Ask her if she knows what to do."

I grabbed the phone from Mom's bedroom.

One call. Then I was going back to my discovery.

CHAPTER SiX

I dialed the number, 231-7132. A palindrome.

> A *pal-in-drome* is something that is the same forward and backward.

The name Bob is also a palindrome. You spell it B-O-B forward and you spell it B-O-B backward. Jay's number is 2317132 forward and 2317132 backward. I don't count the dash because you can't dial a dash.

As the phone rang, I wondered if Jay was home. Maybe he was at his grandpa's or cousin's house. Having a great time.

"Hi," Jay answered the palindrome—I mean the phone.

It surprised me. "Hey, it's Nina. I want to talk to your mom."

"About what?"

"How to get rid of the gum stuck in Kavita's hair."

"I know how."

Did he really know or was he just teasing me? I should have never told him the reason I was calling. "My mom told me to ask your mom. Will you please get her?"

"Peanut butter," Jay said.

I walked back to the bathroom with the phone. "On Kavita's hair?"

"No, on a piece of toast!"

I was annoyed at Jay but I tried not to show it. The last thing I needed was an I'm-almost-done-with-my-assignment and I-know-all-about-how-to-remove-gum-from-hair smart mouth to bug me. I took a deep breath. "May I talk to your mom?"

"Hey, did you finish your discovery?" he asked.

Mom wiped her hand on a towel and stuck it out for the phone. I handed it to her without answering him. Kavita was still showering.

"Hello, Jay," Mom said in her strict voice.

I tried to hear what Jay was saying but couldn't figure out a word.

Jay: "*Gup-sup, gup-sup, gup-sup.*"

Mom: "Are you sure?"

Jay: "*Gup-sup, gup-sup, gup-sup.*"

Mom's eyebrows scrunched together. "You better not be kidding."

Jay: "*Gup-sup, gup-sup, gup-sup.*"

Mom smiled. I don't know why, because Jay couldn't see her. "No, you don't need to come over. Thanks, bye."

Mom handed the phone back to me. "Jay says the gum will come off with peanut butter."

It sounded crazy but Jay knows a lot of crazy facts. Like how much butter goes in a piecrust (½ cup) and how many moons Saturn has. Last year Jay told me that Saturn has 53 moons and 9 more moons are under consideration. If they were all confirmed, Saturn would have 62 moons.

"Nina?" Mom said.

I guess Jay wouldn't lie to Mom. "Okay, let's try peanut butter."

Kavita turned off the shower. "Peanut butter? Yummy!" Kavita stuck her tongue out like a cat lapping an imaginary bowl of milk.

"Not to eat." Mom wrapped Kavita in a blue and pink Cookie Monster towel. Kavita looked puzzled.

I explained. "To rub on your gummy hair."

"Will you do it, Nina?" Mom asked.

"Can I do it later? I'm busy thinking right now."

"Peanut butter rubbing is excellent for inspiring great ideas," Mom said as she dried off Kavita.

"Is that why you apply coconut oil to my hair on Sundays? Do you get great ideas while you rub it in?"

"All the time," she replied.

When Mom rubs oil in my hair, it makes me feel very floppy-relaxy. I never knew it helped her too.

"Okay. I hope I get a great idea like Alexander Fleming. Then maybe I'll discover something important like penicillin."

Mom looked at me. "Penicillin and Alexander Fleming? What do they have to do with your getting ideas?"

"Today we learned about how Alexander Fleming discovered penicillin. I want to discover something. For my project."

Oops! I didn't mean to tell Mom about my project. Maybe all that talk about peanut butter and oil made my mind slippery and it just slipped out.

"Nina, isn't your project due on Monday?"

"Um, yes."

Mom was concerned. "I thought you were done with it. Do you want to discuss it?"

I shook my head. "Don't worry. I still have the whole weekend."

"Is that enough time?"

The last thing I wanted was for Mom to ask me about it fifty times. "More than enough. Once I make my discovery, it will only take an hour to write it."

"That's good to know. And you know what? You made an amazing discovery already."

"I did?"

"Yes, you discovered Kavita. Thank you."

I didn't want to tell Mom that that was not a real discovery. At least not the type I wanted to make. Still,

I was happy I had found Kavita. "You're welcome."

"It was scary to think of our little Kavita in an empty school all by herself."

"I'm not little. Look," Kavita said, coming back to the bathroom.

I didn't know when she had left, but she was now dressed in black sweatpants and a pink sweatshirt. It matched the blob of pink gum tangled up in her black hair. She puffed up her cheeks and leaped into the air. "This is how big I am!"

"That was a big-girl leap." Mom winked at me. It made me feel twinkly and bright like the sparklers we light at the Diwali time.

Kavita sang, *"Big, big, big, I'm as big as a balloon."*

"Nina, while you work on gum, I'll get the dinner ready," Mom said.

I snapped my fingers. "Come on, Kavita. Time for your peanut butter rub."

CHAPTER SEVEN

We all went into the kitchen. Mom handed me the peanut butter and a spoon. She started making dough for rotis.

The peanut butter jar was almost full. I scooped out a spoonful and handed the jar to Kavita. "Hold this."

I used my fingers to push the peanut butter off the spoon and onto her hair, then rested the empty spoon on the jar lid. The peanut-buttery smell was stronger than hair smell, or even dinner smell.

Mom heated up oil with cumin seeds. When she

added frozen peas and corn to it, it made a big *whoosh* sound. Kavita and I loved corn and peas cooked in turmeric and coriander powder. My mouth watered.

As I rubbed the gloppy blob into Kavita's hair, I observed how the sticky, oily stuff was helping take little pieces of gum off.

So far I was not getting any great ideas though. Not yet.

Mom was shredding red cabbage for kachumber. My favorite!

Still no new ideas. I tried to pull the gum out. It didn't work and needed more peanut butter rubbing.

"Hand me the jar, Kavita," I said.

When she did, there was a big hole in the middle of the jar, the size of two fingers.

"Kavita! You've been eating it?"

"*Benot bottor ish for eashing, nosh rubshing,*" she said.

I guess she meant *peanut butter is for eating, not rubbing.* "Not if you have to get gum out of hair," I said. I smeared on more peanut butter.

By now Mom had a bowl full of shredded cabbage. She tossed it with salt and ground cumin and left the bowl on the counter. She put the rest of the uncut cabbage back in the refrigerator. Then she took part of the dough and made a small ball. She dipped the ball into flour, flattened it, and began rolling a roti.

I removed part of the gum from Kavita's hair and wiped it on a paper towel. No new ideas were coming into my head yet.

My arms were getting tired and so was my brain.

Kavita dipped her fingers in the jar again as she sang, "*Gooey, gooey, oily and smelly, my hair is soooo greasy. Gooey, gooey, yummy and sticky, my tummy is soooo happy.*"

At least my peanut butter rubbing was inspiring Kavita, even if it wasn't helping me.

Finally, I got all of the gum out, except for one tiny piece. It was badly tangled up in her hair. And gooey peanut butter covered half of her head.

"Thank you, Nina. I'll get that part out and wash Kavita's hair again," Mom said.

The smell of steamy, yummy puffed roti was making me hungry. "After you're done, can we eat?" I asked, washing my sticky hands in the kitchen sink. "I'm starving."

"I'm not," Kavita said.

"That's because you just ate a whole jar of peanut butter," I said.

"Nope. Only half. My hair ate the other half."

Mom handed me the empty jar to recycle. "Nina, the food is ready. The table is set, so we can eat as soon as I wash Kavita's hair."

She took Kavita to the bathroom. I tasted the kachumber.

It was salty and spicy but not yummy like it usually was. Mom must have forgotten to add something sour. What could I use?

I got out a lemon, cut it up, and squeezed the juice into the kachumber.

I tasted the kachumber again. It was good.

Then I noticed something. The liquidy part at the bottom of the bowl had been purple, but now it had changed color. I took the bowl to the window to make sure my eyes weren't playing tricks on me.

It was true. The cabbage juice had changed from purple to pink.

It was astonishing!

As-ton-ish-ing means you are surprised a ton!

This was it! My PNP! It was my time to ask questions, ponder, and answer them. Time to discover something new and amazing!

What would happen if I added even more lemon

juice? Would it change color again? How would it taste?

My fingers squirmed with excitement. I cut up two more lemons, juiced them, and added the liquid to the kachumber.

This time the juice didn't change color much. And when I tasted it, my tongue and teeth went numb. Now it was too sour. Quickly I dumped the kachumber in the garbage.

I poured dishwashing soap into the empty bowl. The little bit of leftover juice at the bottom changed color again! Now it was blue.

My heart began to thump like my dancing feet—*ta, thi, ta, thi*—and then faster—*ta-thi, ta-thi*.

Maybe this was my great discovery!

But I didn't have time to ponder. I had to make new kachumber before Mom and Kavita returned.

I got out the leftover piece of cabbage and cut it up. I added salt, ground cumin, and a little lemon juice. Just as I was mixing everything together, Mom and Kavita came back in.

"Look, I cut off my gummy hair," Kavita said proudly.

"Why?" Kavita's long hair was shiny and it didn't smell like gum or peanut butter anymore. But now she had a bald spot on left side of her head.

"You wanted me to. Remember?"

"I couldn't get that last piece out." Mom sighed. "I realized we were out of peanut butter so I went to get some coconut oil from our bathroom. When I came back..."

"*Gummy hair, gummy hair isn't as yummy as a gummy bear,*" Kavita sang.

"But her par—"

Mom signaled me to be quiet. She probably didn't want Kavita to think a bald-headed party wasn't fun.

While we ate, I tried not to stare at Kavita's bald spot. "Mom, are you going to the grocery store tomorrow before you pick up Dad from the airport?"

"Yes, I need a few things for the par—uh...afternoon event."

Kavita was busy scooping up peas and corn with a piece of her roti.

"When Dad comes home, I'm going to give him a surprise," Kavita said.

"What surprise?" I asked.

"My bald spot surprise."

I took a sip of water. "That's not a good surprise."

"But he's our dad. He likes all our surprises. Right, Mom?"

"If you say so." Mom sounded tired.

"When you go shopping can you get more peanut butter?" Kavita asked.

"And a red cabbage." I took a second serving of the kachumber.

"You really love kachumber, don't you?" Mom asked.

"As much as Kavita loves peanut butter."

"We have a piece of cabbage left," Mom said.

"Not anymore." I smiled sheepishly. "Plus, I need a whole one. For my discovery."

I told her what happened when I added lemon juice and why I had used up the other piece of cabbage.

Mom looked at the kachumber. "You made this? It's really good."

"Yes. Thank you." Maybe my chopped cabbage was not as fine as her chopped cabbage. But it tasted great.

"I'll buy you two cabbages for your experiment," Mom said. "So you *did* get an idea while rubbing peanut butter on Kavita's head." She served me another warm roti with ghee.

"Yes, kind of." I thought about everything I'd observed during the afternoon.

In-my-head list of what had happened

1. While rubbing peanut butter into Kavita's hair, I watched Mom make kachumber.

2. I tasted the kachumber and realized that something was missing.

3. When I added the lemon juice to the kachumber, I noticed the color change.

4. When I tried to wash the bowl, I saw another color change.

5. Just like Mom, I made kachumber.

None of this would have happened if I had sat in my room and pondered. Or if I had just eaten Mom's *kachumber*. In both cases I would have missed my discovery.

And I wouldn't have figured out how to make kachumber.

CHAPTER EiGHT

After dinner, Kavita and I cleared the table and Mom loaded the dishwasher. Then I brought Sakhi from my room, because the kitchen was filled with things I might be able to use for my PNP.

I crossed out the old observation list and started a new one.

> List of things to add to the cabbage juice
>
> I. vinegar because it is sour like lemon juice (Instead of pink, the vinegar might turn the cabbage juice red. The color of Mom's

lipstick! Maybe I could mix the juice with ghee and sell it as natural lipstick!)

2. soapsuds

3. mango pulp (Mango and red cabbage might be a good combination for a new flavor of juice?)

4. coconut milk (It might be too thick and too white.)

5. spicy curry sauce (That might make a good drink. Instead of spiced latte, Mom and Meera Masi can sip curried cabbage juice.)

I was busy writing when Mom came into the kitchen. "Nina, I need to make an important phone call to a client. Will you keep an eye on Kavita? I'll be in my room."

"But I'm working on my project."

Mom's forehead crinkled. "Kavita's watching an

episode of *Mahabharat,* so she probably won't even move from the couch. Just make sure she stays safe and doesn't go outside."

"I guess Kavita could watch *Mahabharat* for hours without moving," I said. "I'll take care of her."

"Thanks, I'll be done in twenty minutes."

After Mom went to her room, I peeked into the family room. Sure enough, Kavita was sprawled out on the couch watching baby Krishna stealing butter and sharing it with his friends. Soon he was going to get caught red-handed. I wanted to watch that part, but I knew I had to work on my project.

I added to my list.

6.	dal
7.	bitter melon juice
8.	rainwater (if it rains soon)

Suddenly the TV was quiet and Kavita was not. I could hear her crying.

I checked. Kavita lay on the floor, holding her stomach.

"My tummy hurts!" she wailed when she saw me.

"Why didn't you tell Mom?" I asked.

"Because it wasn't hurting five minutes ago."

What could I say to that?

"Lie down." I slipped a pillow under her head. "Better?" I asked.

She shook her head. "I want Mommy."

"We're not supposed to disturb her, but I know what to do," I said.

Mom usually gives us ajvan seeds for stomach-aches. I took out the spice box and scooped up a spoonful of brown seeds. I gave them to Kavita along with a glass of water.

She swallowed the seeds with a few sips of water, then made a miserable face. "I still don't feel good."

"You will in a few minutes."

"Is it a few minutes yet?" she asked.

"No," I said. "All that peanut butter is sticking to your tummy and making it hurt. The ajvan seeds need a little more time to work."

"Will it go away soon? I want to eat my birthday cake."

"You'll be fine," I told her.

She got up.

"Where're you going?" I asked.

"To get a stick of gum."

"No, no. You're not going to chew gum on top of your stomachache."

"If peanut butter takes gum out of hair, then gum should take peanut butter out of my tummy."

"No it won't."

"Yes it will."

Kavita went to the kitchen. I flopped on the couch, holding my head in my hands. If I didn't hold it on, I was afraid it might fall off and roll under the couch.

"Here, I got you a piece of gum too," Kavita offered.

"You want to watch *Mahabharat* with me? It'll make you feel better."

I took the gum. As I chewed I thought, *I can't do any work without a red cabbage, so I might as well watch Lord Krishna getting into trouble.* "Sure, I'll watch."

Kavita scooted up next to me and turned *Mahabharat* back on.

✴✴✴

When Mom was finished with her call, I told her, "Kavita had a stomachache and I gave her some ajvan seeds."

"And it worked," Kavita said. "No more tummy trouble."

Mom hugged each of us. "Should we go get groceries now?" she asked. "It will save us time in the morning."

I didn't want to go, but I needed supplies for my PNP. "Sure. Let's not forget to buy red cabbage."

"And some peanut butter," Kavita added.

Mom held up a piece of paper. "They're both on the list."

We paused *Mahabharat* and left for the store, where we did quick-as-a-snap shopping.

After Kavita and I helped Mom put away the groceries, we unpaused *Mahabharat*. Now that the cabbage was here, I should be doing my work, but I couldn't leave during the very interesting scene that was coming up.

We watched Lord Krishna and his friends playing with a ball. It went into the River Yamuna, and he had to dive in and fight a poisonous snake, Kalinag, to get it out.

When that part was over, Mom said, "Time to call India."

Even though we wanted to watch more, we had to turn off the show. It was important to call India at the right time.

India is far east of the United States, so we always have to think about the time difference. If we don't, we could end up calling our grandparents in the middle of the night.

We are ten-and-a-half hours behind India. It was 9:00 p.m. Friday evening where we were, which meant that it was 7:30 a.m. on Saturday morning in India. (I calculated this very quickly, using this trick: If our time difference was twelve hours instead of ten and half, then 9:00 at night in Madison would be 9:00 in the morning in India. But since it's one and a half hours less than that, it's 7:30 there.)

We called Dad's parents first because they usually get up early. They came up on the phone screen, sitting at the dining table having their breakfast.

"Good morning, Dadi," I said.

"Good morning, Beta," my grandmother replied. "I mean, good evening."

I laughed.

"How was your school today?" she asked.

"Okay." Maybe if she were here, I would have told her about Alexander Fleming's discovery, but it was too hard to do on the phone. "How was your Friday?"

"Tiring. Montu came home with ten friends. He invited them without telling us. We had to make snacks for them and then take them all home. It took half the day."

My cousin Montu stuck his face in front of the camera. He is seven, smack between me and Kavita in age. He took a spoonful of uppma from Dadi's plate and shoveled it into his mouth. I love the fluffy cream of wheat cooked with spices, cashews, and lots of vegetables. I wished I could scoop up some for myself.

"Hi, Nina. When're you coming here?" Montu asked.

"I'm not sure."

"You all should come for Diwali celebration."

"We can't," I said. "We have school."

"All the cousins will be here except you."

I sighed. "I know."

"Dada wants to talk to you," he said, handing the phone over to our grandfather.

"Where did Dadi disappear to?" I asked. Dada adjusted the phone so I could see her as well.

Then Kavita poked her head in front of me and showed them her bald spot. Dadi gasped.

"What have you done, Kavita?" Dada asked.

Before we could explain what had happened, the screen froze and we were disconnected. We called back a couple more times, but it kept freezing. Then we tried Nana and Nani, my other grandparents, but it wouldn't connect either.

Mom looked at the clock. "It's almost time for you two to go to bed. We can try them tomorrow," she said.

Kavita begged, "I want to tell them how I got my bald spot. Please?"

"You can do that tomorrow," Mom said. "You both have dance class in the morning, so you need to go to sleep."

I went to the kitchen for a drink of water and saw the huge new jar of peanut butter on the counter. We must have forgotten to put that away with the other groceries.

I hid it behind the sugar and tea canisters. Hopefully Kavita would never find it.

While I brushed my teeth, I wondered if toothpaste would change the color of the cabbage juice. There was only one way to find out—do the experiment and discover what happens.

My single-track mind was so much on my PNP

report that I forgot to floss. Mom reminded me and I had to go back to the bathroom. While flossing, I wondered what else I was forgetting.

Then I remembered that now Jay was probably my former best friend. It made me sad. I looked at the mirror.

Believe me, flossing and feeling unhappy looks twice as miserable as just flossing or just feeling unhappy. So now I was super miserable-looking.

CHAPTER NINE

The next morning, Kavita and I waited on our front porch with Mom for Meera Masi. Besides being Jay's mom, Mom's friend, and our neighbor, she is also our dance teacher, so we ride to class with her. While I waited, I observed everything around me and made an in-my-head list:

1. The burning bush had gone red.

2. The sun sparkled diamond white.

3. It was a no-wind and no-jacket day.

4. Kavita wore her green knitted hat. It looked

clean. Mom must have washed it yesterday. It didn't match with her blue, breezy, cotton dance outfit though.

5. The sky also wore blue. It matched well with the white cumulus clouds.

"Pay attention in your dance class, Kavita," Mom said. "You have a performance coming up in a couple of weeks."

Kavita pulled her hat down. "I always do."

"Take off your silly hat, Kavita," I said as soon as we got into Meera Masi's car.

"My ears are cold," she replied.

"Oh!" I hoped she was not getting sick.

Dance class started with stretching yoga exercises—cobra, dog, lotus pose, and a few sun salutations. All through it, Kavita kept pulling her hat down.

Finally we were all stretched out, just like Kavita's hat.

We tied bells around our ankles. Now we were ready to dance.

Meera Masi tapped her wooden rod to keep the beat and we began our steps.

Ta, thi thi tat, aa, thai thai tat.

Right, left, right heel, right, left, right, left heel, left, over and over again.

"Arms," Meera Masi said, and we moved our arms in and out and up and down and front and back with the beat.

Once our arms were moving in unison and our bells were jingling together, Meera Masi began tapping faster. Soon we were out of breath, dancing double time.

Then we practiced our group dance to a Bollywood song about a monsoon, fast and exciting. And so much fun!

Then the class was over.

"Wait outside. I'll be with you in five minutes," Meera Masi said to Kavita and me.

The waiting room was packed with aunties and kids. They were not real aunties, but almost-real aunties. Some of them we had known for a long time, some of them we didn't know, but it didn't matter. If they were Indians, we called them aunties. Kavita and I saw our almost-real aunties more than our real aunties who lived in India. The almost-aunties were busy talking to each other, and the kids (almost-cousin kids, though we never called them cousins) were busy playing with each other. It was so warm that it felt like there were a thousand steaming pots of tea in there.

I yanked off Kavita's hat. "It's too hot in here to wear your hat."

"Nina!" she cried.

I gasped. I had forgotten the bald spot.

I stood like a frozen kulfi. Except kulfi is sweet, creamy, and cool, and I felt sour, crummy, and not at all cool.

By the time I recovered from my shock and slipped the hat back on her head, it was too late.

One of the kids pointed at Kavita. "Why do you have a bald spot on your head?"

Someone echoed, "Baldy, bald, bald!"

Kavita's face sagged like a two-day-old balloon.

A couple of the almost-aunties noticed what was

happening and shushed all the kids. The room went quiet. Except now Kavita was crying.

"Kavita, remember how proud you were yesterday after you got rid of the gum from your hair?" I whispered to her. "You were even going to surprise Dad."

Instead of calming her down, my whisper added energy to her crying. "You told me it was a bad surprise! I don't want to give a bad surprise," she said between her sobs. She took off her hat and flung it as far as she could.

It hit Meera Masi in the face as she walked into the waiting room. She grabbed the hat and twirled it in her hand, then extended her other hand to Kavita. "Let's go home."

We were silent in the car.

All the way home.

"Thank you," I said as we got out of the car.

"You're welcome. I will see you both this afternoon. Kavita, I want a big smile for your party."

"Bye-bye," is all Kavita said.

CHAPTER TEN

As soon as we walked in the door, Kavita announced, "Mom, I want to cancel my party."

I guess Kavita left her silent self in Meera Masi's car.

Mom hugged her. "You've been waiting for your party for many months. Now you don't want it?"

"I want a party, but not today," Kavita said.

"You want to postpone it?" I asked.

Kavita wiggled out of Mom's arms. "What does that mean?"

> *Post-pone* means you do it later.

"Like you post a letter to Dadi and it gets to her a few days later. You post your party and do it a few days later."

"Yes," she said. "I want to post my party on a pony and do it later when my hair grows back."

Mom took out a baked potato and peas dish with cheese from the oven. She drizzled it with sweet-and-sour chutney. "Let's talk about the party while we eat lunch."

"Yummy!" Kavita shouted.

I filled glasses with water and Kavita set the table.

Mom dished out a portion and handed it to Kavita. "It's hot, so wait until it cools off before you take a bite."

"Just like I have to wait for my hair to grow before we can have my party."

"Your hair will take a long time to grow out," I said. I took a bite. It was spicy, sweet, and sour all rolled in one. And the cheese made it salty and gooey too.

I wonder what would happen if I mixed sweet-and-sour chutney with cabbage juice. It was thick and dark brown. So even if it worked, I might not be able to see the results. Not a good idea.

"What are you thinking about, Nina?" Mom asked.

"Something about my project," I replied.

"Better concentrate on food now," Mom said.

Kavita was eating and I thought she had forgotten about postponing her party. When she was finished, she picked up her plate and took it to the sink. Then she came back and said, "I want my party in two months. That way no one will tease me 'baldy, bald, bald.'"

Mom's eyes went wide. "What happened?"

"It was kind of my fault," I said. I told Mom how I forgot Kavita was hiding her bald spot and it was so hot in the room that I took off her hat.

I thought Kavita would start crying again, but all she said was, "It's okay. I don't want to have a party with a bald head."

"How about if you wear a hat?" Mom asked.

"I don't want to wear this green one," Kavita said. "It's not a party hat."

Mom turned to me. "Do you still have that straw one with a bow? The one Meera Masi gave you a couple of years ago for your birthday. Remember?"

"Mom, I remember the hat," I said. Even though my mind travels on a single track, I don't forget certain things—like my favorite hat. Since I had caused the baldy, bald, bald teasing problem, it was okay with me if Kavita wore it. Anyway, it was too small for me now. "I know exactly where it is."

"I don't want Nina's hat," Kavita said. She went up the stairs singing, *"Hat, bat, hat, bat, I don't want Nina's hat."*

She kept on singing but we couldn't hear it.

"I bet Kavita wants to make her own hat," I said. "Maybe Dad can help—hey, where's Dad?"

Mom sighed. "His flight was canceled. He won't be home until later."

"We have to take care of a bunch of six-year-olds without Dad?" Even with all his traveling, Dad still tried to be there for our birthdays, the first days of school, parent-teacher conferences, back-to-school nights, and dance recitals. But now he was going to miss Kavita's party.

"Weekend-Only Dad is no fun," I complained. "Even when he comes back on Friday, Kavita and I have dance class on Saturday morning, so we don't see him. Sometimes he doesn't come until Saturday.

And sometimes his flights get delayed or canceled, like today. It's not fair."

"Dad will be done with his Boston project in two weeks," Mom said. "Then he is not going anywhere."

"Really? From a 3.3, we are going to become a 4.0 family?"

"What does that mean?" she asked.

"Never mind. But are you sure he won't be traveling anymore?"

"Yes. I'm sure. Now, if you help me with balloons and setting up, I won't need your help later with the party. Please, Nina?" Mom put her arms around me.

I was so happy about the Not-Weekend-Only Dad news that I said, "Sure." Then I remembered my PNP. "Can I work on my project during the party?"

"Yes. The magician will entertain the kids in the backyard, and Meera Masi will help me with the cupcakes and drinks. Everything will be under control."

I wasn't as hopeful as Mom. Some of Kavita's

friends turn wild when they get excited, just like she does. Avery runs in circles, and Adrian jabbers.

"Okay, everything will be under control," I repeated, just so I could believe it. Then I thought of something. "Jay isn't coming, is he?"

Mom spread a tablecloth on the dining table. "I don't think so. I wonder why he hasn't come over lately."

I shrugged.

I know why, I said inside my head as I stared out the window. I bit my lip so nothing would escape my mouth.

Things that could have escaped from my mouth

* why Jay and I were having problems
* why I didn't want to tell him about my discovery
* why I wanted to compete with him on the PNP

If I mentioned any of this, Mom would be confused. She would want me to explain everything. But I wasn't in an explaining mood. Plus, it would take a long time to answer all the questions she might have. And I had to work on my PNP. Double plus, she was busy with Kavita's party and I didn't want to bother her.

I wanted to keep my fabulous project a secret—from Mom and Meera Masi and especially Jay—until I could write it up and hand it in to Ms. Lapin. And surprise Jay. And Tyler. If I mentioned anything to Mom and she talked to Meera Masi or Jay about it, it would ruin my secret.

So I needed to let Mom think that Jay and I had no problems. At least until after I turned in my PNP.

"Let's finish the rest of the work while Kavita's busy. It'll go a lot faster. Meera Masi will be here soon too." Mom gave me another hug.

She was right. Everything went faster without Kavita. Maybe my discovery would too. If no one is asking you questions, no one is singing at the top of their voice, and no one is nagging you, you might be able to discover exciting and important things. And quickly.

Like Ms. Lapin told us, Alexander Fleming wasn't even looking for penicillin when he discovered it. I bet Alexander Fleming didn't look at the mold for more than a few minutes before he wondered why the bacteria around the mold were dead. He'd discovered an antibiotic by accident because he was observant. Newton saw the apple fall only for a second and he figured out gravity. I was observant with cabbage juice. Now if I asked the right questions, maybe my project wouldn't take much time.

So I had just enough time.

If nothing went wrong.

CHAPTER ELEVEN

Mom and I dragged three card tables and twelve chairs into the backyard.

We have a lot of card tables because Mom and Dad play bridge at our house with their friends. Jay's parents come too, and Jay used to come with them. Sometimes we played board games, colored sheets filled with flowers and plants Mom gave us, watched *Mahabharat* together. Now that I have smashed his ship, maybe he wouldn't want to come anymore.

That made me double sad.

My in-my-heart list

* First, I missed Jay.

* I didn't want him to come today, because I needed to work privately on my PNP and dazzle everyone.

* But I did want Jay to come other times.

* But he might not come over. He probably never missed me because now he got to see his cousins all the time.

It is hard to be sad while you blow up balloons. Sad face is all shriveled up and balloon-puffing face is chubby and cheerful.

I blew up all the balloons. Mom tried to help, but she's no good at it. She can only make them puff up to a size of an apple or a grapefruit. That's it. After that, no matter how much she blows, they stay the same. I think she should be listed in the Guinness World Records as the World's Best Miniature Balloon Puffer.

To get ready for the party

* Mom and I tied streamers and the balloons I had blown up to the mailbox so the guests could find the house.
* I made lemonade for the kids.
* Mom made coffee with steamed milk for her-self and Meera Masi. She put it in a thermos.

How were Mom and Meera Masi going to have a coffee break with Kavita and all her friends running around? Maybe they were counting too much on the magician and his magic.

We were finished getting ready by one o'clock, and the party was supposed to start at two. "Mom, can I get going on my project?" I asked.

"Sure. Thanks for all your help."

I got out the cabbage and other ingredients for my project. "What did you get for party favors?" I asked as I started cutting the cabbage.

"We didn't have to worry about that part. The magician is going to make balloon animals for the kids. He is also going to give them a small magic trick kit."

"Great." I wrote down the steps as I did them.

1.	Chop red cabbage.
2.	Add chopped cabbage and water to a blender.
3.	Blend.
4.	Strain out the liquid.
5.	Put the reddish purple liquid in a pitcher.

Next, I thought about my feelings about this experiment so far and wrote them down.

* Doing experiments makes me feel like a real scientist.
* Observing is like being part of something important.

✽ Preparing everything ahead of time makes me feel organized.

Suddenly I thought, *did anyone else ever discover about the cabbage juice changing colors?* I went to Mom's office and used her computer. I googled "cabbage juice experiment" to see if I could find any information, and 138,000 results popped up!

Oh no! I wasn't the first one to discover this! I felt like a shrinking balloon.

Then I thought.

1. There are more than six billion people in the world.

2. But there are only 138,000 cabbage juice experiment sites.

3. So it was still a very, very special discovery.

I double-clicked the first result. The site was called *Cabbage Chemistry—Science Buddies*. It was very scientific looking. There was a section called *Project Guide*.

The *Cabbage Chemistry* people must like to make lists just like me, because that's what they had done!

It had multiple lists, like:

Getting Started

Doing Background Research

Constructing a Hypothesis

I didn't know what a hypothesis was, so I looked it up. It had a long explanation and sounded science-y to me. I figured out that it meant making a good guess about what will happen.

Good guess means, if you see a furry tail under your bed and hear a meow, you can guess (have a hypothesis) that it will turn out to be a cat. Then you can bend down and look under the bed to investigate. If you see that it is a cat, you know your hypothesis was right.

When I accidently changed the color of cabbage juice, it was a surprise discovery. Now I was planning to do an experiment to see what happens when you add different things to cabbage juice. I was proud of myself for coming up with the experiment on my own and without a hypothesis. They had taken all the same steps I had. They called sour things like lemon juice "acid" and bland things like baking soda "base" and then there was something about pH. The sour things had a low pH and the bland things had high pH. Water was right in the middle. There was a lot more about pH, but I didn't read it. Right now I didn't have time to read more about that or check out the other 137,999 results that had popped up.

I needed to work on my experiment, then write my PNP. Before I got tempted to keep reading, I turned off the computer. That way I could stop googling and get going.

The phone rang. It was Meera Masi. "Nina, is everyone okay?" she asked.

"Yes. Why?"

"Kavita left us a message saying her birthday party

was postpony. Then she went on saying she had posted her party on a pony. Did she mean it is postponed? Or something else?"

Kavita couldn't be doing this! The food was ready, the decorations were out, her friends were coming, and the magician was going to show up soon. She couldn't be making calls trying to change things!

Plus, if Meera Masi didn't come to help, *I'd* have to help and I wouldn't be able to work on my project.

"Oh no, it isn't postpony!" I told her.

"What?"

"Postpony, no, no, I mean it isn't *postponed*. Kavita wanted to postpone it for two months. When her hair grows back. But the party is still on for today. Please come."

"We'll be there."

Meera Masi said "we." Did that mean Jay was coming with her?

I didn't have time to worry about that either.

I hung up the phone and ran to Kavita's room. She

had fallen asleep on her bed with one of the phone handsets by her side. The party list with all the phone numbers was nearby. I picked up the list and the phone and ran out of the room.

Mom was at the kitchen sink, washing grapes and humming a Bollywood tune.

"Mom!"

She put her humming on mute and said, "Nina, I'm glad we called the magician. It cuts down on so much work and hassle. This is almost kind of relaxing." She unmuted her humming button.

"Mom, this isn't the time to hum or relax!"

She jerked around to face me. A grape flew from her hand, hit my cheek, and landed near my foot. "Why? What happened?"

I picked up the grape. "Jay's mom—I mean Meera Masi—called. She had a message from Kavita saying the party was postponed. Mom, Kavita hasn't been making her hat. She's been calling people and postponing her party. Look!" I showed her the list. "She's fast asleep now, but this was on her bed with the phone. She must have called before she fell asleep."

Mom sat down on a chair, looking exhausted. "What—what was she thinking?" she moaned.

"Mom?"

"See if you can find your hat while I call people. I just have to go down the list because I don't know who Kavita has called. I need to reinvite them all," Mom said. "I'll let Kavita sleep for another twenty minutes or so."

I shook my head. "I've caused a lot of problems for Kavita, but I didn't mean to. If I hadn't said that her bald spot wasn't a good surprise for Dad, she would have been fine."

Mom patted my head. "It's not your fault. You've been a great help. Everything will work out."

I ran to my room. My hat was in one corner of my closet. My giant stuffed beaver, Lucky, was wearing it.

When I picked up the hat, I noticed my sweater in another corner. I went closer and sniffed. It still didn't smell moldy. Mold was slow to grow and I needed to leave it there. It wouldn't help me for my PNP, but it still might lead to super-mold and cure people of diseases, so I wouldn't give up yet.

I carried the hat to Mom. She was on the phone.

"No, no. The party is today," she said. "Yes, the same time. What? They went to a movie?" She listened and then said, "I understand. I hope you can reach them and they can make it to the party."

Mom turned off her phone and threw up her hands. "After all this work, paying for that clown—"

"I thought you called a magician."

"Magician or clown, what difference does it make now? We'll be lucky if all the kids show up. Looks like Kavita called them right after lunch. While we were getting ready for her party, she was calling it off."

"Postpony," I said.

Mom gave a baby smile. Then her frown took over. "Avery's family already made other plans. Now they have to change them again."

"Are we still having my party?" Kavita asked from the doorway.

How long had she been standing there?

"Yes, we are," I said.

"But I already sent it away on a pony. Postpony, remember?"

"You cannot postpone your party without telling me," Mom said in a stern voice. "That's not allowed. I have called all your friends back and some of them will start arriving in a few minutes. So get ready." Then she must have remembered it was Kavita's birthday party, because she added, "Sweetie."

"I want my bald spot to go away," Kavita whined.

"It will," Mom said. "Don't worry about your hair. All your friends are excited to celebrate and have fun with you at your birthday party."

"No!" Kavita stomped her foot.

"Would you like to wear this for your party?" I held out my hat.

"The pink-bow hat?" She broke out in a grin.

Ding-dong, the doorbell rang.

Mom went to the door. It was Meera Masi.

Alone.

Even though I missed Jay, it was good that he wasn't here. Now I could get my PNP done. And then surprise him with my dazzling discovery.

Yes!

I led Kavita upstairs to her room. She carried the hat like it was a crystal vase.

"Let's see if it fits you," I said. I took the hat from her hand and placed it on her head. "It looks great. Now let's find a dress to go with it."

"I'm already dressed," she said.

"You're going to wear sweats with a fancy hat?"

"It's my birthday party, so I get to choose."

"So you choose to wear a sweat suit?"

"No, I choose not to change my clothes."

I threw up my hands.

CHAPTER TWELVE

Now that Meera Masi was here, Mom didn't need my help and I got right to work. I made some changes from my original PNP supply list because I didn't know if we had vinegar. We had lemonade for the party, so I thought I could use some of that. I decided the curry sauce was red and it would be difficult to tell the color change, so I left it out.

My revised list

1.	lemonade
2.	dish soap

3. laundry detergent

4. baking soda

5. coconut water

I labeled small paper cups and filled them with the things I wanted to add to the cabbage juice. That way I wouldn't get the different ingredients confused and as soon as the party started I could get going on my discovery.

It was twenty minutes to two. I poured myself a glass of lemonade and sat at the kitchen counter, looking over my list to make sure I hadn't missed anything.

"Have you finished your PNP?" a gravelly voice asked.

Startled, I spat out my lemonade. I turned my head to see Jay standing there, grinning.

"Where is everyone?" he asked in a normal voice.

So he didn't come to see me. He came for Kavita's birthday treats! I picked up a napkin to clean up the lemonade. "They'll be here soon. At least, some of them will be." As I wiped the counter, I slipped my list under the napkin holder.

Mom came into the kitchen. "I could use another cup of coffee. What about you, Meera?"

"You have to ask?" Meera Masi followed her in. "We still have a few minutes before the party starts."

At the mention of the coffee, Jay took out a mug from the cupboard.

"No coffee for you," Meera Masi said.

"But I didn't have lunch. I'm hungry," he whined.

"Then you better have some food."

"If you want roti, there're a couple left over from last night," Mom said.

"Yes! Thanks." Jay opened the stainless-steel container on the counter and placed two rotis on a plate. Then he stuck his head in the refrigerator, grabbed a bottle of spicy mango lemon pickle, and placed it on the counter.

"Sure, Jay, make yourself at home," I said. As soon as I said that, I wished I had stayed quiet. Jay was here, acting like he used to when we were best friends. That was a good thing and I had ruined it.

But he ignored what I had said.

"So what do you want to do?" Jay asked, as if this were his home and not mine. It must be from habit. When he was little, he practically lived at our apartment. Then last year, we bought this house, on the same street as his family, so we were always going back and forth.

I sighed. "I have to do my homework."

"PNP? I'm finished with it."

"Sure. The whole world knows it."

He spread pickle over one roti, placed another on top, and rolled them together into a mini baton. "Not bragging. Mom made me work on it. She told me if I wanted to go fishing with Jeff and Grandpa tomorrow, I had to finish all my homework today."

"Oh." I twitched with jealousy. I wished I had cousins here to visit. I wished my grandparents lived close by so I could spend a week or even just a night with them. India is so far away and it's so expensive to get there, I've only been there once. We often do virtual visits, but that's not the same. When your family is thousands of miles away, you can't do certain things.

My in-my-heart list of what you can't do when you are many miles away

* hold your grandparents' hands
* share yummy uppma with your grandparents like Montu does

* play with your cousins
* say "good morning" to your family when it is morning or "good night" when it is night where you both are
* make your sister play with a cousin so you can have a sister break

When you are far away, all you can do is stare at their faces on a screen that keeps freezing and miss them even more.

"Did you write up your grand discovery?" Jay asked, narrowing his eyes.

Jay's bitter-melon eyes by themselves are intimidating.

In-tim-i-dat-ing means it makes you feel not as good as that person.

When his eyes turn sharp like that, they become double-intimidating.

I looked away. I was caught. He was here and I had to work on my project. I couldn't keep it a secret from him. "Not yet," I mumbled.

"How come?"

Before I could answer, Mom and Meera Masi walked back into the kitchen. "It's almost two. Since we're getting a magician, I told the parents to drop the kids off. They should arrive any minute," Mom said.

Meera Masi nodded. "The party will be fun. We just have to make sure Jay doesn't eat all the cupcakes."

Jay lifted up his roti baton. "Mom, can I have a little coffee to wash this down?"

"Wash it down with a lot of water instead," she said.

"Or some lemonade or juice," Mom suggested.

Jay took the pitcher of cabbage juice out of the fridge. *Was he going to drink it?*

I slid him the mug he had taken out for coffee.

"Thanks," he said.

"You're welcome." Since I had a whole pitcher of cabbage juice, I didn't mind sharing some with him.

I couldn't wait for him to take a sip.

He was just about to when Kavita ran into the kitchen, holding onto her hat. "Is the magician here yet? I want him to come before my friends come."

"Why don't you watch for him from the front window? He'll be here any minute," I said. I didn't want anything to interrupt Jay's juice drinking.

The phone rang. Mom picked it up.

"Hello? Yes...what?" she asked. She sighed, then said, "I'm sorry to hear that. Thanks for calling. We'll find another way to entertain the kids. I hope you feel better."

She hung up the phone. Her face looked all crumpled up, as if she was about to cry. "The magician got food poisoning, so he can't be here," she announced.

"Why can't he make the poison disappear?" Kavita asked. "He must not be a real magician."

"Mom, what are you going to do?" I asked. "It's a disaster."

Di-sas-ter means a change or surprise that you are not happy about.

"All I can say is that I'm glad that not as many children are coming now. Still, we better find a way to entertain seven kids for two hours."

"With Kavita, that's eight kids and we have them for hundred and twenty minutes!" I blurted.

"Maybe you and Jay can help," Meera Masi said.

This was supposed to be my time.

MY.

TIME.

By now Jay had gobbled up the rotis and mango lemon pickles. Since the magician wasn't coming, Meera Masi wanted Jay and me to entertain Kavita and her friends for two hours. So I guess the magician had gobbled up our afternoon.

When was I going to do my report?

I must have looked miserable because Mom said, "Nina's supposed to work on her special project."

Why did Mom have to tell everything to the whole world?

"Jay, how come I haven't seen you do one?" Meera Masi asked.

"I'm already done." Jay's green eyes darted from my mom to his.

"Mom, Avery is here," Kavita called. "I see her car."

Mom and Meera Masi left the kitchen.

"Still working on your discovery?" Jay asked. My fingers curled up into a fist, but I didn't reply.

I tried to slide my list out from under the napkin holder, but Jay saw it.

"What's that?" He grabbed it and read aloud: "Lemonade, dish soap, laundry detergent—"

I stopped him. "Jay, I'm doing an experiment using all these things."

"Like I did for the science fair last year?"

"Huh?"

"Remember, I had this pH experiment with cabbage juice and it changed color from yellow to red depending on how basic or acidic the stuff was?"

"I wasn't there. I was sick—"

"With flu, I remember."

I felt so dumb.

First, I had been so excited about my discovery.

Then 138,000 hits popped up when I typed "cabbage juice experiment." That meant at least 138,000 people had done it before. Actually, a lot more than 138,000 people had done it.

Still, that had been okay. Because I was going to write about how red cabbage kachumber had led me to this experiment and how I repeated it and made observations.

But now I found out Jay had already done the exact same experiment in third grade.

I was not okay anymore.

I snatched my list away from Jay. It tore.

"Hey, stop," he said. "We can work on it together."

"You already did it last year," I said. "In our school. In front of everyone. Including Ms. Lapin. Now I don't have anything special to write about." I pushed back tears.

He picked up his mug. I held my breath. He put it back down without taking a sip. Now that we had talked about the cabbage juice, he might figure out that he was about to drink some. I wanted to see look on his face when he took a sip! That would make my sad tears turn into laughing tears. If he didn't take a sip, then I was going to be double sad.

"Why are you staring at me like that?" he asked.

"I'm deciding if I'm sad or not."

He shook his head, then picked up the mug again. He took a huge gulp before his face scrunched up all weird. He ran to the sink.

I moved out of his way, just in case. He spat it out.

I couldn't stop laughing, and happy tears rolled down my cheeks.

"You tricked me," Jay said.

"I didn't. You poured the juice yourself. You just assumed it was grape or cranberry."

"Who has a pitcher full of cabbage juice?"

"You could have looked at the color, you could have smelled it, and you could have asked questions. Then you'd have discovered it was cabbage juice."

"Yes, Scientific Nina," he said.

"Don't call me names. I don't have my discovery or my PNP."

"So? It isn't my fault!" he snapped.

Meera Masi opened the screen door and hollered, "Come on, you two! We really could use some help."

"I can't," Jay said. "I'm disappearing from here."

She gave him a look. "Use your magic and appear in the backyard in five minutes. Both of you."

We stood there for a second. Magic-frozen.

Then I thought of something. "Jay, let's do the experiment in front of Kavita and her friends! It'll be like a magic show."

His eyes brightened. "You have all the stuff on the list ready?"

"In the laundry room. We can dress as magicians!"

He looked annoyed. "Not doing that."

"Why not? It'll be fun. And I know exactly where to find magicians' clothes!" I ran out of the kitchen.

He followed me.

In Dad's closet we found an embroidered velvet cap and silk kurta shirt for Jay to wear. While he got dressed, I ran to my room and changed into a langha outfit of a long skirt and blouse with a matching sparkly scarf.

We ran back down to the kitchen. "I'll grab the other things from the laundry room." I handed the cabbage juice pitcher to Jay. "Just in case you get thirsty."

"Not funny," he said.

We carried everything outside.

When Meera Masi saw us in our outfits, she beamed. *"Arre wah!"*

"Instead of one magician, we have two," Mom announced to the kids. Even with Kavita's "postpony," phone call, her seven friends had showed up.

The kids stopped running around. They looked at us as if we were from another galaxy. Then they settled down at the card tables.

I placed the cups of lemonade, dish soap, laundry detergent, baking soda, and coconut water on the table.

"Ready?" I whispered to Jay.

"Ready."

CHAPTER THIRTEEN

"Abracadabra, *jadu manter, choo manter*! Want to see some magic?" I asked the kids.

"YES!" they all called out.

Jay poured cabbage juice into a clear plastic cup.

"What color is this?" I asked the kids, picking up the cup.

"Purple!" everyone shouted, including Mom and Meera Masi.

"I can add one magic potion and change the color." I clapped. "Assistant, bring me the first magic potion."

Jay didn't move. "I am not your assistant," he growled.

"Just play along," I whispered. "Hand me the lemonade."

I turned back to the kids. "Sorry. My assistant is kind of lazy."

Everyone laughed.

Jay bowed. "Sorry, Master." He handed me a cup. "Here you go."

"Now watch the color in this cup turn from purple to pink. Abracadabra, *jadu manter, choo manter*," I said, moving my arm in a slow circle. Then I dumped some liquid from the paper cup into the cup of cabbage juice.

"That's not pink! That's blue!" Kavita shouted.

"My master doesn't know the difference between pink and blue like you do," Jay said.

They giggled.

I frowned. That Jay! He had switched lemonade with dish soap.

Jay poured some cabbage juice into a fresh cup. "Now watch this carefully," Jay said to the kids. He added some lemonade and swirled the mixture.

"Now it's pink!" the kids shouted.

"I didn't need to say those silly magical words, did I?" he asked.

"NO!" several shouted.

I picked up one of the cups. "Here! Here! There's magical power in this magical powder. It'll make pink turn blue," I said.

I took the cup from Jay and sprinkled in a tiny amount of the baking soda.

I closed my eyes and chanted, "Moon dust, moon dust, make your magic."

I twirled around as I swirled the cup.

The liquid turned blue.

From the wide eyes of the audience, I could tell that they were impressed.

"Green is my favorite color. Can you make it green?" Kavita asked.

Jay took off his velvet cap and placed it on my head. "Time to show off your magic."

I whispered, "I don't know how to make it green."

He turned around. "My master doesn't know how to make it go from blue to green, but I, the real Master Magician, can do anything."

He took the cap off my head and put it back on his. "This time I'll say the silly magic words and it will still work. Abracadabra, *jadu manter, choo manter!*" he shouted and dumped more of the white powder in the glass. Then he covered the glass with his cap and walked around in a circle.

When he took off the cap, the liquid was green. Kavita and her friends applauded like he was a royal magician.

"Am I not the Master Magician?" he asked.

"YES!" the kids shouted.

"How did you do it?" I asked him.

"How did you do it?" Kavita and her friends echoed.

Jay smiled. "I can turn it green because I have green eyes."

"I've got blue eyes. I can turn it blue!" Avery rushed up and tried to pick up the juice pitcher.

I grabbed it before she could.

Instead, she snatched the cup of magical powder—I mean baking soda—and ran off.

Kavita chased her, shouting, "You can't take the magician's stuff! You can't take the magician's stuff!"

Other kids sprang up from their chairs and began chasing Kavita and Avery.

"Avery, Kavita, sit down," Mom said.

"Help us," Meera Masi said to Jay.

"What do you want me to do, tackle them?" he asked.

I ran after Avery and caught her. I grabbed the paper cup, but she held on to it tightly. Then suddenly she let it go and the powder sprayed.

All over me.

"Stop it, Avery!" Kavita said.

"Did you get it in your eyes, Nina?" Jay asked.

"I don't think so."

"Then you are fine."

I glared at him.

"Just remember. It was your idea to do a magic show," he whispered.

Someone whistled. "Everyone! Get back in your seats," Meera Masi said. "Please."

After they had settled down, Mom said, "Magicians, please continue with the show."

"From a magician to a ghost," Jay said, sweeping his arm toward me.

"I want to be ghost, I want to be a ghost!" someone shouted. I think it was Zachary. Anyway, he fell out of his chair and landed on the grass.

Jay straightened the chair, picked Zachary up, and planted him back on it.

"Don't excite them too much," Mom whispered to Jay and me.

We took turns changing the color of the cabbage juice some more. When we were done I said, "Abracadabra, *jadu manter, choo manter!*"

Jay said, "Our show is done. Let's chant the magic words."

The kids chanted, "Abracadabra, *jadu manter, choo manter*!"

We bowed.

They clapped. Mom and Meera Masi gave us a standing ovation. Although I guess they were already standing when they started clapping.

While they served cupcakes and lemonade to everyone, Jay and I snuck back into the kitchen.

"How did you change the juice from blue to green?" I asked Jay.

"Because of my green eyes."

"No way. You did it by dumping in more baking soda," I said.

Jay smiled. "You figured it out."

"Want a cupcake?" I asked him.

He frowned. "Only one cupcake? After all the work I did?"

I slid three across the counter.

Before we could eat, Mom rushed in. "We have to figure out the party favors!"

"Mom, do we have to think of everything?"

"Yes. Well, no. But yes, right now you do." Mom huffed. "The magician was going to give us favors, but now that he didn't come, we don't have anything to give to the kids."

"While the kids eat the cake, I can run to the grocery store and buy some candy for party favors," Meera Masi said.

"How about also giving them a red cabbage to use to do the experiment at home?" I asked.

"I have the steps for the experiment on my computer. I can print copies," Jay said.

"Title it *Magician's Juice*. They can do the magic at home. And if they're too lazy to do the experiment, they can eat the cabbage," I said.

"Excellent idea," Mom said.

Before he left, Jay grabbed his nonmagician clothes. "Are you going to write up this experiment for PNP?"

"No. How can I? You already did it in third grade."
I was a mixture of sad and disappointment.

Dis-ap-point-ment means how sad you feel when your plans don't work out.

"Oh."

Doing the experiment with Jay had been fun, though. So much fun that I had forgotten about my PNP. And so much fun that Jay had forgotten about being mad at me. But all the fun we had was going to end now.

Sometime soon, Jay would go back to being my former best friend.

But maybe, just maybe, he wasn't even mad at me? Could that be true?

I wished I could ponder about it more. But I certainly didn't have time.

Because, by Monday, I had to finish my PNP.

CHAPTER FOURTEEN

I slumped like a grumpy doll. I didn't eat my cupcake.
I didn't change my clothes. I just sat in my magician's
outfit and watched Kavita and her friends stuffing
their mouths with food. Kavita had forgotten about
her bald spot and was talking and laughing.

When Meera Masi came back with candy and red
cabbages, I helped her fill the party favor bags. Jay got
back and slipped in his two-page instructions titled
Magician's Juice into the bags.

Finally the party was over and I went to my room.

When the breeze came in through the window, the pieces of paper on my desk fluttered. My list! I had taken it out when I came to my room to transform into a magician. I tore the two pieces up even more and threw them in my trash can. Then I felt bad, so I fished out the pieces and dumped them in the recycling bin.

I changed clothes and sat on my bed, holding my stuffed beaver and thinking of my great discovery that was never going to happen.

But with or without a discovery, the Personal Narrative Project had to happen.

And I had nothing to write about. Tears came rushing to my eyes.

"Nina?" Jay called from outside my door.

I stayed quiet.

"NINA?"

I wiped my tears. "Come in."

"Wasn't that fun?" Jay asked, coming in.

"Fun. Yeah."

He looked at me. "What happened?"

"Nothing. Well not nothing. I still don't have my PNP and soon you'll be mad at me again."

"What? Mad at you again? What's that supposed to mean?"

"Mad. Like you were after I broke your pirate ship."

"I was just upset when it happened."

"You—you weren't mad at me all this time?" I asked.

He shrugged. "No. I got an A and I didn't have to finish painting all those pirates. It would have taken me a long time."

"Really?"

"Yes, really! How come you thought I was mad?"

"Because you didn't come over like you used to. So I thought we weren't friends anymore," I said.

"You thought we weren't *friends* anymore?"

I nodded.

"Ready to go, Jay?" Meera Masi hollered.

He looked confused. "You worry too much."

"What's that supposed to mean?"

"You figure it out." He left without explaining.

Now I was confused. What had just happened? I pondered. Then I made a list in Sakhi.

After pondering list

* Jay seemed surprised that I thought he was mad at me.

* Then he seemed annoyed when I told him I thought we weren't friends.

* When he said, "You figure it out," he wanted me to think about our friendship.

✳ What did he want me to realize?

It was almost like an experiment. I had to think about the conclusion of our talks.

I made one more list!

✳ Maybe I had been feeling so bad about smashing his pirate ship that I assumed Jay was mad.

✳ Maybe I had become more sensitive to his teasing.

✳ Maybe I worried so much about our friend-ship changing that I accidentally changed it.

✳ Maybe it never really changed or maybe that's why Mom and Meera Masi acted as if nothing had happened.

✳ Maybe I worry too much.

✳ Just like Jay said.

CHAPTER FIFTEEN

I closed Sakhi. Now that Kavita's party was over and Jay was gone, I still had to work on my PNP. I had to write about something boring and bland about my life and would never get a good grade. It was so unfair!

Even though Jay was my friend, I would still have to hide my bad grade and embarrassment from him. Maybe I could turn into a real turtle and hide in my shell?

That made me laugh.

Before I started on my project, I went to the kitchen to get a glass of water. Mom was wiping the countertops and Kavita was peeling red cabbage leaves and eating them. I didn't tell her not to eat them. They were probably good for her.

"Thanks for all your help today, Nina," Mom said. "You and Jay did a wonderful job. I was thinking maybe when Dad gets home we could all go out for dinner. You pick the place."

The phone rang. "I'll get it," Mom said.

By "all" did Mom mean the Davenports too? Meera Masi and Jay had also helped. I hope Mom invited them too. I crossed my fingers.

Kavita reached for a jar of peanut butter.

"You're not spreading that stuff on the cabbage leaves," I said.

"Okay," she said. Then, before I could say anything, she took a blob and smeared it on her hair.

I filled my water glass. "What are you doing?"

"I want to discover something, like you did." She put her hand in her pocket and took out a piece of well-chewed bubblegum from a wrapper. She stuck it in her hair where she had smeared the peanut butter. "I'm going to discover what happens if you stick gum on peanut-buttery hair."

"Why do you drive everyone crazy?" I asked.

"You want me to drive you boring?"

I didn't answer.

Instead I went to my room, took out a piece of paper, and wrote:

✳ *I have nothing to write about.*

I crossed out that thought because that track was not taking me anywhere.

✳ ~~*I have nothing to write about.*~~

✳ *My great discovery.*

The red cabbage wasn't my great discovery. So many people had already done the pH experiment, including Jay. I crossed out that one too.

✳ ~~*I have nothing to write about.*~~

* ~~My great discovery.~~

* *Discover something in the next few hours and write about it.*

I wasn't going to be that lucky. Since yesterday so many things had happened, which left me no time for a discovery.

In-my-head list of all that had happened in the last two days

1. I left Kavita at school.

2. She had gum in her hair.

3. We got rid of the gum.

4. She still ended up with a bald spot.

And today wasn't any better. It definitely was not my lucky day. The morning started off wrong.

1. I pulled off Kavita's hat.

2. She got upset and didn't want her party.

3. Dad's flight was canceled, so I had to help Mom.

4. Kavita tried to postpone her party.

5. Jay told me he had done the pH experiment last year.

6. The magician got sick.

7. Jay and I had to become magicians.

Jay and I didn't do too badly as magicians, though. I think we were good. Maybe we could start our own business. Now that I knew he wasn't mad at me, we could work together.

That idea made me smile.

I sat looking out over the backyard. Mom and Meera Masi had cleaned it up, but the grass was crushed where the tables and chairs had been and where kids had run.

I felt like that trampled grass. I knew I'd spring back up as soon as I had my Personal Narrative Project done.

I took a fresh sheet of paper and started a new list of possible PNP topics.

1. How I lost (and found) my sister
2. How with Jay's help we solved the gum-in-hair challenge
3. How I accidently exposed my sister's bald spot
4. My not-so-great red cabbage kachumber discovery
5. Nina and Jay: The Magnificent Magicians
6. Why Jay Davenport is still my best friend

I crossed out the last one. I wasn't going to write about Jay and show it to Ms. Lapin. But the other five things had promise. Now I had to choose one of them and start writing.

After pondering a bit, I took a long drink of water. Then I picked up my pencil and wrote.

I used to think that my life was as exciting as a bland rice cake. I was wrong. My life is as delicious as a bowl of kachumber: crunchy, spicy, salty, and sour.

Then I made a list of the reasons why I thought so:

* Even though my dad travels a lot, Mom and Dad take care of everything Kavita and I need. From red cabbage to peanut butter, from laundry to hugs. They are steady, strong, reliable, safe. So they are like a bowl of shredded cabbage. Without shredded cabbage there wouldn't be any kachumber. Without Mom and Dad there wouldn't be our family.

* Once Dad forgot to pick us up. I exposed Kavita's bald spot and really upset her

even though I didn't mean to. We all make mistakes and sometimes we make each other upset; that's like squeezing a little lemon juice in the bowl of cabbage.

* My mom always has interesting things growing in the garden, but never in the refrigerator. That's like another squeeze of lemon juice.

* My sister sings made-up songs. They just sprout out of her mouth. Some are good, some are terrible. But most of them are ridiculous. Kavita's songs are so ridiculous that they make me laugh. She adds extra crunch to my life.

* I have a best friend from before I was born. We laugh together, we tease each other, sometimes we trick each other and

compete with each other. Every once in a

while, we get mad at each other. But no

matter what, I can't imagine life without my

best friend. He is like salt in the kachumber.

Kachumber wouldn't taste good without salt.

Without my friend my life wouldn't feel good.

✳ Here is a snapshot of one day of my

kachumber life.

Then I wrote down everything that had happened during the last twenty-four hours. (Except for my sleeping time. Nothing ever happens when I sleep.)

I finished my report before Dad came home, and we had dinner at the Pasqual's restaurant with the Davenport family.

It was a perfect ending to a perfect day.

Tomorrow I had a whole day to spend with my 4.0 family.

On Monday, I would hand in my PNP and surprise my not-former best friend with my dazzling project.

And if some super mold likes unwashed sweater and started growing, I could have Ninacillin soon. That would end all my competition with Jay. Because just like Alexander Fleming, I would become an unforgettable discoverer.

Here is a list of things
people have said about Nina Soni.

"I adore Nina and know readers will, too."
—Debbi Michiko Florence, author of
the *Jasmine Toguchi* series

"A perfect fit for readers who enjoy realistic fiction about
friendship and self-discovery."
—*School Library Journal*

"...a flawed but refreshing and very likable protagonist..."
—*Booklist*

Available in hardcover,
paperback, and ebook

Available in hardcover,
paperback, and ebook

Available in hardcover,
paperback, and ebook

She's a phenomenon!

Phe-no-me-non means a happening or an event.